TV stars . . .

"Congratulations," said Mrs. Armstrong. "I heard you two are television stars."

"That's right," Jessica said. "See?" she whispered to me. "I told you we were stars!"

"I guess you're right!" I replied.

"Make sure you act like a star," Jessica said.

"What do you mean?" I asked.

"People don't want television stars to act like everyone else," Jessica explained.

"How do they want them to act?" I asked.

"Different," Jessica said. "A little better than everyone else."

I didn't really want to act better than everyone else. It didn't sound like fun. But Jessica knew more about being a star than I did. I decided to give it a try.

Bantam Books in the SWEET VALLEY KIDS series

SWEET VALLEY KIDS

THE JESSICA AND ELIZABETH SHOW

Written by
Molly Mia Stewart

Created by
FRANCINE PASCAL

Illustrated by
Ying-Hwa Hu

BANTAM BOOKS
NEW YORK • TORONTO • LONDON • SYDNEY • AUCKLAND

RL 2, 005-008

THE JESSICA AND ELIZABETH SHOW
A Bantam Book / January 1995

*Sweet Valley High® and Sweet Valley Kids are
trademarks of Francine Pascal*

Conceived by Francine Pascal

*Produced by Daniel Weiss Associates, Inc.
33 West 17th Street
New York, NY 10011*

Cover art by Susan Tang

ISBN: 0-553-48205-X

Published simultaneously in the United States and Canada

Bantam Books are published by Bantam Books, a division of Bantam
Doubleday Dell Publishing Group, Inc. Its trademark, consisting of the
words "Bantam Books" and the portrayal of a rooster, is registered in the
U.S. Patent and Trademark Office and in other countries. *Marca
Registrada.* Bantam Books, 1540 Broadway, New York, New York 10036.

PRINTED IN THE UNITED STATES OF AMERICA

0 9 8 7 6 5 4 3 2 1

To James Peter Nardi

CHAPTER 1

A Big Audition

Hi! I'm Elizabeth Wakefield. I am seven years old.

I have a twin sister. Her name is Jessica. We're *identical* twins. That means we look just like each other.

Jessica has blue-green eyes. So do I. Jessica and I both have long blond hair with bangs. We also have a lot of clothes that match. When Jessica and I wear the same outfit, nobody can tell who is Elizabeth and who is Jessica. It's funny! Sometimes we can even fool Mom and Dad and Steven.

Steven is our big brother. He's two

years older than me and Jessica. Steven thinks he's great. We think he's a big pain.

Jessica and I go to Sweet Valley Elementary School. We're in the second grade. We sit next to each other in Mrs. Otis's class.

I love school. I even like homework. My favorite subject is reading. That's because I'm going to be a writer when I grow up. Jessica doesn't like the learning part of school. She likes recess and lunch and seeing her friends.

I have lots of friends at school, too. My favorite friends are Amy Sutton and Todd Wilkins. I like Todd even though he is a boy. Jessica doesn't like boys. Her best friends are Lila Fowler and Ellen Riteman.

On the playground, my friends and I pretend we're space explorers or scientists at a jungle outpost. We play tag, too. That's my favorite! I hardly ever have to be It.

Jessica never plays tag with us. She doesn't like games that make you sweaty. Jessica likes jump rope, hopscotch, and the swings.

Sometimes people are surprised that Jessica and I are so different. They think we should be the same *inside* because we look the same on the *outside*. That's silly. Every person in the whole world is different inside.

But even though we like different things, Jessica and I are best friends. Jessica loves being a twin. So do I. Well, at least most of the time. See, Jessica has one bad habit. She's always getting me into trouble.

"I have some exciting news," Mrs. Otis announced one morning at school. "Sweet Valley Cable Television is starting a show for kids. They want a second or third grader to host the program. Tryouts are next Monday at their studio."

"Let's try out!" Jessica whispered to me.

"I don't know. . . ."

"Come on, Lizzie," Jessica begged. "Please, please, please! Pretty please!"

"OK, OK," I agreed.

I didn't want to be on television. I was busy with soccer and riding lessons already. But it's hard to say no to Jessica. I figured it was easier to go to the tryouts than to argue about it. Besides, I was sure the TV people would never pick us.

On the Monday of the tryouts, Mom drove us to the studio. She took Ellen and Lila, too. The other girls were excited. I just wanted the tryouts to be over. I was afraid they would make us sing.

"I'll be back to pick you up later," Mom promised.

I followed Jessica, Lila, and Ellen into the studio. The waiting room was packed full of kids. Practically everyone was talking at once.

"Does my hair look OK?" Jessica asked.

Lila wrinkled her nose. "Not really."

"Let's go to the bathroom," Jessica said. "I want to fix it."

Ellen and Lila agreed.

"I'll wait here," I said. I didn't care what my hair looked like.

Jessica, Ellen, and Lila disappeared into the crowd.

I sat down on a bench. The girl next to me was reading *Kangaroo Campers*, by Angela Daley.

"Hey!" I exclaimed. "That's one of my favorite books!"

The girl smiled at me. She had long black hair and big brown eyes. She was wearing a Lakers sweatshirt and leggings. "It's one of my favorites, too," the girl said. "I've already read it three times."

"Why are you reading it again?" I asked.

"Because these tryouts get so boring!"

"Do you come to a lot of them?" I asked.

"At least one a week."

"Wow!" I was impressed.

"I made a cereal commercial last fall," the girl told me.

"What cereal?"

"Double Chocolate Chip Minis," she said.

I made a face. "I don't like that cereal. It's so sweet, it gives me a headache."

"Tell me about it! I had to eat twelve bowls the day we made the commercial."

"My name is Elizabeth," I told her.

"I'm Jane," the girl said. "Is this the first time you've gone out for something? I've never seen you at tryouts before."

I nodded. "It was my sister's idea. I don't want to be famous, but she does."

"Don't worry," Jane said. "Even if you get the part, you won't be too famous. The show is going to be on Channel 31."

I giggled. "We don't even get that channel."

"You have to have expanded cable," Jane said.

Jessica, Lila, and Ellen came back, and I introduced them to Jane. Soon an important-looking woman arrived. She had white-blond hair. She was carrying a clipboard.

"My name is Linda," the woman announced. "I'll be the producer of the program. I hate to waste time. So I'm going to send some of you home right now."

Linda strode down the middle of the room. "You can go," she said, pointing to a girl. "And you . . . and you . . . and you."

7

A couple of the kids groaned. One boy looked like he was going to cry.

"Stay, stay, stay," Linda said, pointing at Ellen, Lila, and Jane.

"All right!" Lila whispered.

Linda studied me and Jessica.

Jessica poked me.

I tried to smile sweetly.

"Twins," Linda said thoughtfully. "Interesting. Stay."

By the time Linda got to the end of the room, she had sent half the kids home.

"That was fast!" I exclaimed.

"Television," Jane said with a shrug. "How you look is very important. Linda didn't think those kids looked right."

That seemed unfair to me, but Jessica didn't care. "At least we look good enough to stay," she said.

Jane was called into Linda's office before the rest of us. She came out about five minutes later. "Good luck," she told me as she gathered her things together.

"Thanks," I said. "Same to you."

Pretty soon it was Jessica's turn. She was gone about a second. Then she came back. "She wants to see us together!" Jessica told me excitedly. I jumped up and followed her into the office.

Linda was sitting behind a big, messy desk. "Names?" she asked.

Jessica and I told her our first and last names.

"Phone number?" Linda asked.

We told her.

"How old are you?"

"Seven," I answered.

Linda took our pictures with a Polaroid camera. "Thanks, girls."

"That's it?" Jessica asked. "Don't you want us to sing for you?"

"No, thanks," Linda said.

"We could dance," Jessica offered.

"No," Linda said firmly. "I've got all I need."

Jessica was crushed. "We didn't get it," she decided as we left the office.

I was glad.

CHAPTER 2

Good News

The next day, Mom made us cinnamon toast and apple slices for an after-school snack. Yummy! I was eating my second piece of toast when the phone rang. Mom went to get it.

"Girls, it's for you," she announced.

Jessica didn't get up. So I went to the phone.

"Hello?"

"Hello," came a voice. "This is Linda from Sweet Valley Cable."

"Oh. Hi." I remembered that Linda was the woman with the clipboard. But I didn't know why she was calling.

Maybe we had left something at the studio.

"I have exciting news," Linda said. "You've been chosen to be the show's host!"

"Me?"

"Well, you and your sister," Linda said. "Your first show is tomorrow. Please be at the studio by three thirty. We'll go on at four o'clock."

"Tomorrow?" I asked, surprised. I didn't know the show was going to be so soon. "Don't we need time to rehearse and stuff?"

"No rehearsing," Linda said. "It just makes you stiff."

"But how will we know what to do?" I asked.

"You can do anything you want," Linda said. "You could talk about school, books, sports, or movies, for example. Why don't you make a list of things that sound fun?"

"What if we can't think of enough stuff?" I asked.

"Don't worry," Linda said. "I have some ideas."

Linda told me some other stuff, too. She said the show would be on three days a week: Mondays, Wednesdays, and Fridays. It would be half an hour long. And it would be called *It's the Jessica and Elizabeth Show!*

The show would be live. That meant people would see it at the same time we were doing it.

When I got off the phone, I told Mom and Jessica the good news. "Linda is going to call you later," I added to Mom.

Jessica started jumping up and down and screaming. "Let's go to the park! I want to tell everyone!"

"OK," I agreed. I was almost as excited as Jessica. Linda had picked us over all those other kids. It was unbelievable!

Jessica and I rode our bikes to the park.

Amy was playing tag with Eva Simpson and Winston Egbert. Lila and Ellen were on the swings.

Eva and Winston are in Mrs. Otis's class, too. Winston has big ears. Eva is really fun. She's on my soccer team.

"Everyone, come quick!" Jessica yelled.

Our friends gathered around.

"Guess what?" Jessica said.

"Your parents are sending Steven to school in Alaska," Ellen suggested. Ellen knows how annoying big brothers can be. Her sister is almost as bad as Steven.

"Wrong!" Jessica shouted. "We got it! Elizabeth and I are going to be on television."

"Wow," Amy said. "You guys must have been really good at the tryout."

"That didn't have anything to do with it." Lila sniffed.

15

"What do you mean?" Jessica asked.

"You got picked because you're twins," Lila said.

"You don't know that!" Jessica said angrily.

"Then how come Linda took both of you?" Ellen asked. "She was looking for only *one* host until she saw you guys. It's not fair! I wish I had an identical twin."

"Come on, you guys," Eva said. "Don't be sore losers."

Lila and Ellen didn't say anything more. But they still looked mad.

"Are you excited?" Amy asked.

"I'm nervous," I told her. "Linda said we get to decide what to do. Do you guys have any ideas? I brought a piece of paper to write them down."

"I have an idea," Winston Egbert said. "You could tell jokes."

I frowned. "I don't know any jokes."

17

"I always forget them," Jessica agreed.

"I know lots of jokes," Winston said proudly. "What's fat, gray, and has sixteen wheels?"

We all thought for a few seconds.

"What?" Lila finally asked.

"A hippo on roller skates!" Winston said.

The rest of us groaned.

Winston was laughing. "What do you get when you cross a cow with an earthquake?"

"What?" I asked.

"A milkshake!" Winston said.

That one made me giggle.

Not Jessica. "We're not going to tell silly jokes like that on our show," she said.

Winston shrugged. "I can tell you a lot more if you change your mind."

Even though Jessica didn't like them, I wrote down the two jokes Winston had told us.

"Any other ideas?" I asked.

"You could do a movie review," Eva suggested.

"Good idea," I said. "But I haven't seen a movie in a long time."

"I saw *Tommy's Terrific Trip* last weekend," Eva reported. "It was great! But the little boy sitting behind me and Dad cried at the end. I think it's too scary for little kids."

I wrote that down as fast as possible. The other kids kept talking.

"You could talk about homework," Lila suggested.

"Homework?" Jessica stared at her. "Why would we talk about that?"

"Let me finish!" Lila said. "I was trying to say you could talk about why teachers should give *less* homework."

"Hmm," Jessica said. "That's not a bad idea."

By the time we went home, I had a

long list of ideas. Our friends had been very helpful.

Jessica and I ate dinner. Then we talked about what to do on our show until it was time for bed.

CHAPTER 3

Here's . . . The Twins!

"**A**re you OK, Elizabeth?" Mom asked the next afternoon. "You're awfully quiet."

Mom had picked me and Jessica up at school. She was driving us to the studio for our first show.

Jessica was bouncing up and down in her seat. "Aren't you excited?" she asked me.

"No," I said. "I'm too nervous."

"How come?" Jessica asked. "We're going to have so much fun! This will be even better than the piano recital. Lots more people will be watching!"

Jessica loves to perform. She started taking piano lessons just so she could play onstage. But I thought being on television sounded scary.

Mom pulled up in front of the studio.

Jessica immediately opened the door and jumped out of the van.

I took my time.

"Just do what Linda tells you," Mom told me with a smile. "Everything will be fine. I'll pick you up right here after the show."

"OK, Mom," I said, climbing out of the van.

Mom watched until Linda let us into the studio. Then she beeped the horn and pulled away.

"Hi, girls," Linda greeted us. "Take a seat. I'm in the middle of talking to Hank. He's going to be answering the phones for us this afternoon. I'll see you in a few minutes."

Jessica and I sat down. The studio

was very quiet. It almost didn't seem like the same place where we had tried out.

The doorbell rang.

"Get that!" Linda yelled from somewhere farther inside.

I answered the door. It was Jane.

"Hi," she said.

"What are you doing here?" I asked.

"I'm your understudy," Jane announced.

"What's an understudy?" I asked.

"Elizabeth!" Jessica said. "Don't you know anything?"

I shrugged. "I don't know what an understudy is."

"It means Jane will go on if one of us gets sick or something," Jessica explained.

"Oh," I said. I felt kind of bad. Jane knew much more about television than we did. She should have been the host.

But Jane didn't seem mad. "How are you feeling?" she asked.

"Fine," Jessica said.

"Nervous," I said.

"If you get shaky, take some deep breaths," Jane suggested. "That will calm you right down."

I took about a million deep breaths in the next half an hour. "Where's Linda?" I kept asking.

Linda didn't come to get us until a few minutes before four o'clock. "It's time for you to get on the set," she said when she finally appeared.

The set was two armchairs on a platform. A piece of blue material was tacked up behind the chairs.

"Sit down," Linda commanded.

We sat.

Linda pinned a tiny microphone to Jessica's shirt. She pinned another one to my shirt.

"We're going to run a phone number

on the screen," Linda told us. "Hank will answer the phone out in the hall. He can talk to me through this."

Linda tapped the side of her face. A piece of plastic was pushed into her ear. It looked just like a hearing aid.

"Hank will tell me when we have a caller," Linda went on. "Jane and I are going to stay in here. But once the show starts, the viewers will be able to hear anything that is said in this room. So Jane and I aren't going to speak. When I have something to tell you, I'll write you a card."

Jane pointed to a tall stack of cardboard. "Um—you guys do know how to read, don't you?" she asked.

I nodded. There was a lot more I wanted to know. But there didn't seem to be time to ask questions.

"Lock the door," Linda told Jane.

Jane turned a big bolt. Then she walked over and stood next to Linda.

Linda was messing with a big camera on wheels. A red light came on. Linda pointed a finger at us.

Jessica and I looked at each other and shrugged.

Jane was mouthing something to us.

I squinted at her. What was she trying to tell us? And why didn't she just *say* it?

"What?" Jessica finally asked.

Jane shook her head.

"You're on!" Linda whispered.

Jessica looked panicked for a second. Then she smiled and said, "I'm Jessica!" just the way we'd planned.

"And I'm Elizabeth!" I added.

"Welcome to our show!" Jessica and I said together.

My heart was pounding. I was sure everyone in TV-land would see my chest moving up and down. But after our first mistake, things improved.

We told all of Winston's jokes. We

complained about homework, just as Lila had suggested. We warned everyone not to take little kids to *Tommy's Terrific Trip*.

I was beginning to relax. Being on television was actually kind of fun. Still, I felt as if the show had been going on for hours. I figured we had only a few more minutes to go. Even though I was having fun, I was relieved that the show was almost over.

Linda wrote out a sign. She tried to hold it up and work the camera at the same time. But she was holding the sign at a strange angle. I couldn't read it.

Jane came forward and took the sign. She held it up. The sign read TWENTY MINUTES TO GO.

My jaw dropped. When you're on television, half an hour is a really, really long time.

Jessica and I had already done everything on our list. We looked helplessly

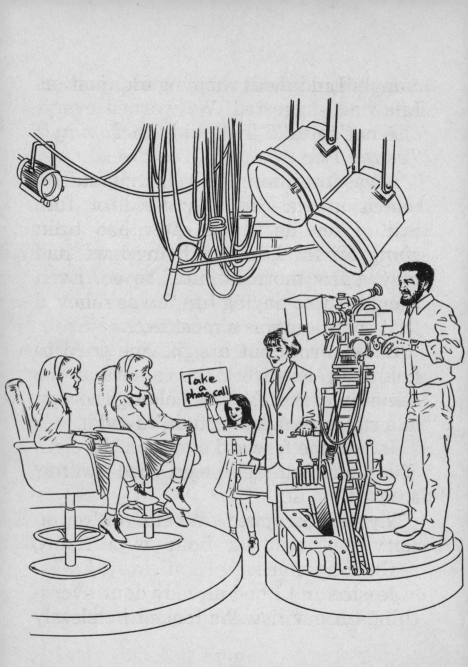

Take
a
phone call

at Jane. Linda was working on another sign.

"What's next?" I asked Jessica.

TAKE A PHONE CALL, the card read.

"Why don't we take a phone call?" Jessica asked. She sounded like the host of one of those afternoon talk shows. Then I realized. She *was* the host of an afternoon talk show! And I thought being on TV was fun again.

"Hi, my name is Mattie," came a voice out of nowhere. "Where do you guys go to school?"

Jessica told Mattie about Sweet Valley Elementary School. I told her about Mrs. Otis.

We took three more calls after Mattie's.

Then Linda wrote SAY GOOD-BYE on a sign.

"Good-bye," I said right away. I was exhausted.

"Thanks for watching our show,"

Jessica added. "We'll be back again on Friday." She was much better at being on television than I was.

The red light on the camera went out. Jane clapped for us.

"How did we do?" I asked Linda.

"Lousy," Linda said. "That was the worst show I've ever produced."

Jessica's face fell. I felt disappointed.

Linda pushed a few buttons on a very fancy VCR. "Here's a videotape of the show. Watch it. And try to think of some ways to improve."

"Don't listen to Linda," Jane said as we waited for our rides. "You did a great job. Especially for your first time."

CHAPTER 4

Good Reviews

Mom pulled up in front of the studio about two minutes after Jane's mother. Jessica and I climbed into the van. "Hello, girls!" Mom said cheerfully.

"Hi, Mom."

"Hey."

"You don't sound very happy," Mom said. "Didn't you have a good time?"

"It was OK," I said.

"Linda told us we were lousy," Jessica said.

"She did?" Mom frowned. "Well, maybe you should wait and see what your friends thought."

"All right," Jessica and I both answered at the same time.

A few minutes later, Mom pulled up in front of Amy's house. Amy's mother is a television reporter. She has to watch the news all the time, so the Suttons have expanded cable. That means they get Channel 31. So do lots of other kids at our school.

Amy had invited a bunch of kids over to watch our show. As we climbed out of the van, the Suttons' front door opened. Amy, Lila, Ellen, Eva, Winston, Todd, and Steven ran out.

"You were great!"

"That was such a cool show!"

"You squirts weren't *terrible,*" Steven added.

I glanced at Jessica. She looked just as surprised as I felt. We had been a hit!

"What part of the show did you like best?" Jessica asked.

"The jokes were funny," Winston said.

"The best part was when you talked about homework," Lila said. She looked grumpy. "And that was *my* idea!" I thought Lila was still mad that she hadn't gotten to be host.

"I liked the movie review," Eva said.

"What else?" Jessica asked eagerly.

"My favorite part was the very beginning," Todd said. "You know, when you pretended not to know what was going on."

Winston nodded. "That was funny."

"For a while, I thought you guys really did mess up," Todd went on. "But then I realized it was just a joke."

"But we really—" I started.

Jessica pinched me. "That part was *my* idea," she said.

I didn't think Jessica should lie. But then again, maybe it was OK. Our friends were so impressed with us. In a way, they were our fans. I didn't want to disappoint them.

We had a great time at Amy's. I felt proud. My friends said lots more nice things about *It's the Jessica and Elizabeth Show!*

When we got back to our house, Dad was already home from work. "How did it go?" he asked us right away.

"It was great," Jessica said.

"We were a hit!" I added.

Dad grinned. "This calls for a special celebration dinner. What would you girls like to eat?"

"Pizza!" Jessica and I both yelled.

"Me too," Steven added.

"Being on television really *is* fun," I whispered to Jessica.

She grinned. "I told you so!"

CHAPTER 5

Overnight Sensations

"Hurry up, Jessica!" I yelled up the stairs the next morning. "We're going to miss the bus!"

I was holding my lunch bag. My milk money was in my pocket. My finished spelling homework was tucked into my books. I was ready to go to school. But Jessica didn't come down the steps.

I'm always on time. Jessica never is.

Mom came into the front hall. "Don't worry," she said. "I already told Jessica I'd give you kids a ride to school. You must be tired out after yesterday."

I wasn't tired at all. But I love getting a ride to school. "Thanks, Mom!" I said. Then I ran upstairs to see what Jessica was doing.

Jessica was in our room. She was pulling on her favorite pink sweatshirt. She had a pink ribbon in her hair.

"Why are you getting dressed up?" I asked. "We don't have a show today."

"No," Jessica agreed. "But everyone will be watching us in school. I want to look pretty."

"Why would people be watching us?" I asked.

"Because we're stars," Jessica said.

"Stars?" I repeated.

Jessica nodded. "Want to wear a ribbon in your hair, too?"

"No, thanks," I said. I thought Jessica was being silly. We had been on television only *once*. That didn't make us stars. But when Mom dropped us off at school, I started to wonder. A group of kids were waiting to talk to us.

"Tell me all about the show!" Caroline Pearce demanded. Caroline is in Mrs. Otis's class. She's a busybody. She has to know everything that everyone in our class does.

Jessica smiled at Caroline. "It was fabulous."

Lois Waller was there, too. "Hi, Elizabeth," she whispered. Lois is very shy. "I just wanted to tell you that you were great yesterday."

"Thanks," I said.

Lois and I followed Caroline and Jessica into school. Tom McKay and Sandra Ferris, two more kids from our class, trailed behind us. They wanted to hear about the show, too.

Mrs. Armstrong, the principal, was standing in the front hallway. "Congratulations," she greeted us. "I heard you two are television stars."

"That's right," Jessica said. "See?" she whispered to me as we walked toward Mrs. Otis's room. "I told you we were stars!"

"I guess you're right!" I replied.

"Make sure you act like a star," Jessica said.

"What do you mean?" I asked.

"People don't want television stars to act like everyone else," Jessica explained.

"How do they want them to act?" I asked.

"Different," Jessica said. "A little better than everyone else."

"Better?" I repeated. "I don't think—"

"Haven't I been right about everything so far?" Jessica interrupted.

"Yes," I admitted.

After class started, I thought about what Jessica had said. I didn't really want to act better than everyone else. It didn't sound like fun. But Jessica knew more about being a star than I did. I decided to give it a try.

"Who has something for Show and Tell?" Mrs. Otis asked the class.

Jessica raised her hand.

Andy Franklin raised his hand, too. Andy is good at math. He wears glasses. Jessica says Andy is a nerd, but I like him. Mrs. Otis called on Jessica.

"Yesterday, Elizabeth and I hosted our own television program," Jessica announced. "I brought in a tape of it."

"How long is the show?" Mrs. Otis asked.

"Half an hour," Jessica said.

"That's too long for Show and Tell," Mrs. Otis said. "But we can see the beginning."

Jessica gave Mrs. Otis the tape.

Mrs. Otis unlocked a closet. She wheeled out the television and VCR. The class sat in a half circle around the television. Mrs. Otis popped in the tape.

40

Guess what? Mrs. Otis played the entire show! After it was over, she let everyone ask us questions. Show and Tell took a long time.

Everyone had fun. Well, everyone except for two people. One was Lila. She was still mad that it wasn't *It's the Lila Show!*

The other was Andy Franklin. When we were going back to our seats, I noticed that he looked angry.

"What's wrong?" I asked him.

"You took up all of Show and Tell," Andy said. "It wasn't fair. I had something I wanted to show, too."

"What?" I asked.

"My bug collection," Andy said. "I just found a really neat beetle."

"I'm sorry," I said.

"Don't worry," Jessica said a little while later when I told her about Andy. "People don't want to look at bugs. They're disgusting."

I knew Jessica thought bugs were disgusting. But I was pretty sure some other kids in the class liked them.

"How do you know what everyone thinks?" I asked.

Jessica shrugged. "I'm a TV star."

"That's right," I said. "And so am I!"

Later, Mrs. Otis let me and Jessica lead the class to the lunchroom. I liked walking at the front of the line. It made me feel important.

Jessica and I ate lunch with Amy, Julie Porter, Lila, and Ellen.

"My mother bought me a magazine about horses," Amy announced.

"Neat!" I said. "Can I see it?"

"Sure," Amy said. She pulled out her magazine. But before I could look at it, two fourth-grade girls came up to our table.

"Aren't you Jessica and Elizabeth?" the dark-haired girl asked.

"Yes," Jessica said.

"Your show was terrific yesterday," the girl said.

"I saw it, too," her friend added. "It was really funny."

"Thanks," Jessica and I both said.

"Well, see you around," the older girls said.

"I can't believe it!" Jessica exclaimed when they were gone.

I was surprised, too. "*Fourth* graders watched our show!"

"We must be really good," Jessica said. "We're attracting a very mature audience."

Lila rolled her eyes. But the rest of our friends nodded.

Jessica and I talked about our show while we finished eating. I forgot all about Amy's magazine. She looked disappointed when she put it away. I promised to look at it the next day.

We went out to the playground. Jessica and her friends started to jump rope.

"Let's play hopscotch," Julie suggested.

"I want to play tag," I said.

"We played tag yesterday," Julie pointed out.

"I know," I said. "But it's more fun than hopscotch."

"That's not fair!" Julie said.

Julie was right. But Jessica had said to act better than everyone else. Didn't that mean I should always get what I wanted?

I shrugged. "*I* think it's fair."

"Come on," Amy said. "Let's play tag. I'll be It."

I smiled.

Julie looked upset. Usually that would have bothered me. But today I was just happy I had gotten my way. That's what TV stars are supposed to do.

CHAPTER 6

Television Experience

"What do you want to wear?" I asked Jessica on Friday morning. Our second show was that afternoon.

"Something really fancy," Jessica said. "How about our peach dresses?"

"The ones we wore to that wedding?" I asked.

Jessica nodded.

"OK," I agreed. I started to look through our closet.

Jessica was brushing her hair.

Steven ran down the hall. "You squirts better hurry," he said. "The bus will be here in about two minutes."

Jessica and I didn't hurry. Television stars never rush.

A few minutes later, Mom zipped into our room. "What are you girls doing? Why aren't you dressed? Steven already left for the bus!"

"Aren't you going to drive us to school?" Jessica asked.

Mom raised her eyebrows. "I wasn't planning on it."

"You weren't?" I asked.

"Why would I drive you?" Mom peeked out the window. "It's not raining. And you don't have anything heavy to carry."

"Well, we can't just ride the bus," Jessica said.

"Why not?" Mom asked.

"Our fans would bother us all the way to school," I explained.

Mom made a funny noise. It sounded almost like a laugh.

"I'm sorry if your fans bother you," she said. "But you still have to ride the bus. I don't have the time to drive you to school every day. Now hurry up and get dressed."

"This is so uncool," Jessica said after Mom left.

I felt kind of bad. "Well, Mom *is* busy. And I usually like to ride the bus."

Jessica frowned. "It's all wrong for our image."

"You mean people don't want to see television stars riding the bus?" I asked.

"Exactly," Jessica said. "We're above that."

"What are we going to do?" I asked.

"I'll explain to Mom," Jessica said. "I'm sure she'll see things our way."

Mom looked surprised when Jessica and I came downstairs. "Why are you wearing your best dresses?" she asked. "Is today school picture day?"

"No," Jessica answered. "We just want to look pretty."

Mom glanced at her watch. "Well, it's too late for you to change now," she said. "And you already missed the bus. Get into the car."

Jessica tried to talk to Mom on the way to school. "We really can't ride the bus, you know," she said.

"Oh, yes, you can," Mom said.

"But—" Jessica started.

"I'm not going to discuss this," Mom said. "You'll take the bus to school from now on. Period."

When we got to school, nobody was waiting out front for us. "Where are our fans?" I whispered to Jessica.

"They must be inside," Jessica said.

They weren't in the hallway. I started to get worried. But as soon as we got into Mrs. Otis's room, Ellen ran up to us. "I have an idea for your show," she announced.

Jessica and I hadn't talked about what we were going to do on that afternoon's show. I was glad Ellen had a suggestion. But Jessica put her nose up in the air.

"We don't need your help," Jessica told Ellen. "Right, Elizabeth?"

I thought about it for a second. "Well, *we're* the ones with television experience," I reminded Ellen.

"Fine," Ellen said. She stomped away.

"What's the matter with her?" Jessica asked.

I shrugged.

It was a boring morning at school. Everyone else seemed to be talking and laughing. But they never came over to talk to me. No one even asked any questions about our show. I was happy when it was finally time for recess.

"Want to play tag?" Todd and Kisho Murasaki asked me on the playground.

I almost said yes. But then I started to wonder. . . . Was playing tag right for

my image? I thought about how Todd gets all red and sweaty when he runs around. Yuck.

"No, thanks," I said. "Jessica and I have to go to the studio right after school. I don't want to get dirty."

Kisho and Todd looked surprised. I never used to care about getting dirty. But that was before I was a *star*.

Todd shrugged.

"See you later," Kisho called.

The boys ran off.

I looked around the playground. Eva was playing with the boys. Julie and Amy were playing hopscotch. They hadn't even asked me if I wanted to play.

Lila and Ellen and Jessica were near the swings. It looked like they were arguing about something.

I sat down on the wall and watched the other kids play.

After a while, Jessica came over and sat with me. Recess was a little lonely.

51

CHAPTER 7

Too Far

"What's next, Jessica?" I asked brightly.

Jessica shot me an angry look. "Let's take a phone call."

It was later that same afternoon. Jessica and I were on the set of *It's the Jessica and Elizabeth Show!* The show had been on for only about fifteen minutes. But Jessica and I had already run out of things to talk about.

Linda shook her head. "There are no calls," she mouthed to us.

"Um," Jessica said, "why don't we . . ." Her voice was beginning to sound shaky.

"We'll take a call later," I said as smoothly as possible. This was a disaster! I wished we had listened to Ellen's idea. Linda was writing out a card. A second later, Jane held it up. It read TALK ABOUT YOUR FRIENDS.

"Elizabeth is my very best friend," Jessica announced.

"And Jessica is my best friend," I added.

Linda made a face.

Jane motioned that we were making her sick to her stomach. I was getting angry. It isn't easy to think of stuff to talk about for a whole half-hour! Jane and Linda had some nerve to complain.

"Of course, we have other friends, too," I said.

Jessica nodded. "My other best friend is Lila Fowler."

Linda scribbled quickly. TELL US SOMETHING SHOCKING ABOUT LILA, her next sign said.

"Um . . . Lila lives in a huge house," Jessica said slowly.

"She has a maid," I added.

"And a swimming pool," Jessica said.

There was a pause.

Linda motioned for us to go on.

"Lila sleeps with a night-light," Jessica blurted out.

"Even though she's seven years old!" I added.

Linda gave us a thumbs-up sign.

Jessica was starting to warm up. "Once," she said, "I caught Lila cheating at hopscotch."

"You did?" I gasped. "I didn't know that!"

"What secrets do *you* know about our friends?" Jessica asked.

I thought about it for a minute. I couldn't come up with anything really good. Still, I had to say *something*. "Well, you know how Todd Wilkins thinks he's such a superjock?"

Jessica nodded.

"OK," I said. "Get this. At our last soccer game, Todd was standing right in front of the goal. I passed the ball to him. It should have been easy for him to kick it in."

"What happened?" Jessica asked.

"Todd ran toward the ball," I told her. "But instead of kicking it, he *stepped* on it. The ball rolled, and Todd ended up flat on his face in the mud! His nose was bleeding, and then Todd started crying. What a baby!"

On the day of the game, I hadn't thought Todd's accident was funny at all. I had been worried about him. Now I was laughing pretty hard.

So was Jessica.

Linda was working on another sign. This one said GO TO THE PHONE.

"We have a phone call," Jessica said.

"Jessica?" came an angry voice.

I stopped laughing. It was Lila!

"Oh . . . hi, Lila," Jessica said.

"I have news for you!" Lila shouted. "You're not my best friend anymore. I'm never, ever talking to you again! You sleep with a stuffed koala!"

"Well, you sleep with a unicorn!" Jessica shot back.

"You are such a baby!" Lila yelled. "You never deserved this show in the first place."

"You're just jealous!" Jessica hollered.

"Come on, you guys," I said. "Don't fight."

I was too late. Lila had slammed down her phone.

"You'd better tell Lila you're sorry tomorrow," I said to Jessica.

"Oh, be quiet," Jessica said. "You sound like Mrs. Otis."

"Don't get mad at me!" I said.

Linda was holding up the GO TO THE PHONE sign again.

"We have another phone call," Jessica said.

"Elizabeth, can you hear me?"

I gulped. "Hi, Todd. Yes, I can hear you."

"I'm surprised," Todd said. "I didn't think snakes had ears!"

My jaw dropped. "I'm not a snake!"

"Yes, you are!" Todd yelled. "You're a snake and a—a stupid girl! And you're not my friend."

"I don't want to be your friend!" I shouted.

"Good," Todd said.

"Good," I answered.

Todd hung up.

"You'd better say you're sorry to Todd tomorrow," Jessica said smugly.

"Be quiet," I said.

Linda was holding up the SAY GOOD-BYE sign.

"Thanks for watching," Jessica said sweetly.

57

"See you on Monday," I added. I was happy when the red light on the camera went out.

"Wow," Jane said. "That was some show."

"I'm glad Mom wasn't watching," Jessica said.

"I'm so sorry," I told Linda. "I can't believe we were fighting with our friends during the show!"

"I'm sorry, too," Jessica said.

"Don't worry," Linda said. "I liked it."

"Really?" I asked.

"Sure," Linda said. "It was spicy. I bet our ratings will go through the roof!"

Jessica and I traded surprised looks.

"That was exactly the kind of show I want to see," Linda went on. "I'm really proud of you guys."

"Watch out, Hollywood!" Jessica said. "Here we come!"

Jane was quiet while we waited for our rides. Jessica was too happy to notice, but I finally asked Jane what was wrong.

"Well, aren't you guys worried?" she asked. "Your friends sounded really mad."

"I don't like to fight with my friends," Jessica explained. "But if it makes me famous, maybe it isn't so bad."

CHAPTER 8

Mad

Jessica and I didn't tell our parents much about our second show. We thought it was great. But we knew Mom and Dad wouldn't agree.

We played at home all weekend. We didn't go to the park because Lila and Todd would be there. They wouldn't understand that TV stars have to worry about ratings, not about their friends.

I saw Todd on the bus on Monday morning. I hoped he had finished being mad.

"Hi," I said.

Todd looked out the window. He didn't say anything.

"Hi, Ellen." Jessica tried to sit down next to her friend.

Ellen quickly put her books on the empty seat. "This seat is taken," she said. "I'm saving it for a friend."

"I'm your friend," Jessica said, sounding surprised.

"No, you're not," Ellen said. "You were mean to Lila."

"Find a seat!" the bus driver yelled.

Jessica and I found two seats next to each other. Caroline Pearce was the only person who talked to us. She asked what other secrets we knew.

"How was your show on Friday?" Mrs. Otis asked when we got to her room.

"Spicy," I said.

"Really?" Mrs. Otis asked.

I nodded. "We could tell everyone about it during Show and Tell."

Andy Franklin ran up to us. "You promised I could show my bugs today!" he reminded Mrs. Otis.

"Bugs are boring!" I burst out.

"Are not!" Andy said.

I stuck my tongue out at him.

Tears sprang to Andy's eyes. "I don't like you anymore," he told me. "You're acting just like Jessica."

"At least Jessica's not a crybaby!" I shouted.

"That's enough," Mrs. Otis said. "Elizabeth, please sit down."

Mrs. Otis let Andy show his bugs. A lot of kids pretended to be interested. Jessica and I sat in the back and whispered.

When it was time to eat, Jessica asked Mrs. Otis if we could lead the class to the lunchroom.

"Not today," Mrs. Otis said. "It's Lila's turn."

Lila smiled proudly. She sent me and

62

Jessica to the end of the line for whispering. Then she marched to the lunchroom like she was the Queen of Sheba.

Jessica and I sat by ourselves in the lunchroom. There was lots of room at our table, but nobody sat with us. Our friends all sat smushed together at one table.

"Everyone is mad at us," I told Jessica.

"They're not *mad*," Jessica said. "They're jealous."

That made sense. Everyone must have been wishing they were us. Why else would they be mad?

"Lila is the most jealous of all," Jessica added.

I giggled. "I'm surprised she hasn't turned green!"

Jessica and I finished eating. We went out to the playground. Todd and Kisho were playing tag with a bunch of other kids.

I ran up to them. "Can I play?"

"No," Todd said. "We don't play with snakes."

"Besides," Kisho added, "you might get dirty!"

Jessica was sitting on the wall. I sat next to her.

I watched Julie and Amy play hopscotch. They looked like they were having a good time. Tag is more fun. But I decided I would play hopscotch if Amy and Julie asked me.

They didn't ask.

CHAPTER 9

Viewer Feedback

"I have to talk to you," Linda said on Monday afternoon. Jessica and I had just arrived at the studio.

"So talk!" Jessica snapped. She was in a crabby mood. I don't think she liked everyone being jealous of us.

"We got a letter from one of your fans," Linda said. "Actually, I guess she isn't a fan anymore."

Jane was standing near Linda. She looked worried.

I plopped down in my seat on the set. "Why not?"

"This viewer was pretty upset about

Friday's show," Linda explained. "She thought you girls were much too nasty."

"But you liked the show," Jessica said.

"I changed my mind," Linda said. "I want you to be nicer this afternoon."

"Because of one letter?" Jessica asked.

"It's the only letter we received," Linda said. "So just be nice."

"I liked it better when you were nice, too," Jane piped up.

"OK," I said. I could be nice. But I was really thinking about something else. "Hey, Linda?" I asked. "How come our show is called *It's the Jessica and Elizabeth Show*? Why not *It's the Elizabeth and Jessica Show*?"

Jessica shot me an angry look.

"I don't know." Linda walked over to the camera and started fiddling with it. "I just thought it sounded better."

"I don't think that's fair," I told Linda.

"Then we'll change it," Linda said.

"Good!" I sat back in my chair, satisfied.

"No way!" Jessica yelled.

"*Yes* way," I said. "I'm older than you are. My name should come first."

"Elizabeth . . ." Jane whispered.

"It was my idea to try out for the show," Jessica argued. "My name should come first."

"Jessica . . ." Jane said in a very low voice.

"Big deal," I said. "Besides, 'E' comes before 'J' in the alphabet. So my name should come first."

"You guys . . ." Jane said in a loud whisper.

"What do you want?" Jessica yelled.

Jane pointed to the camera. The red light was on. Everyone had just heard me and Jessica fighting.

Jessica and I calmed down. We started the show. But I was still mad.

About ten minutes later, we took a call.

"You two look so much alike," the caller said. "How do your friends tell you apart?"

"I'm the smart one," I replied.

Jessica gave me a furious look. "But I'm the *popular* one," she said smugly.

"That's not true!" I shouted. "I have just as many friends as you do."

"Oh, sure," Jessica said. "Everyone thinks you're a goody two-shoes!"

"Am not!"

"Are too!"

Linda was holding up a sign. It read BE NICE!

Jessica and I didn't pay any attention.

CHAPTER 10

Linda Dives In

"**I**'m just as smart as you!" Jessica yelled.

Linda put down her BE NICE! sign. "Girls!" she shouted. "I'm giving you until the count of three to calm down. One!"

Jessica and I should have been surprised. Linda had never talked during the show before. But we were too angry to care.

"If you're so smart, how come I get better grades than you do?" I asked Jessica.

"Two!" Linda shouted.

"Because you're a teacher's pet!" Jessica said. "*Some* people have better things to do than homework."

"Three!"

"Better things?" I repeated. "Like what? Play that stupid piano until we all go crazy?"

Linda marched onto the set. "That's enough!" she yelled. "I'm producing this show. You kids will do what I say!"

The light on the camera was still on.

Jessica stared at Linda. So did I.

"I asked you to be nice," Linda reminded us. "But you wouldn't do what I asked. And so . . . so, I want you out of here! Jane will host the next show."

"You can't do that," Jessica said. She looked like she was about to cry.

"I can and I will," Linda told her.

"What about our fans?" I asked.

"They've already forgotten about you," Linda said.

She stomped off the set, got behind

the camera, and glanced at her watch.

"We have one more minute," Linda said. "Say good-bye."

Jessica looked at the camera. She took a deep breath. "Good-bye," she whispered.

"Thanks for watching," I added quietly.

Linda turned off the camera. The show was over.

"Get out of here," Linda said. "I'll call you when I want you. *If* I ever do."

Jessica and I got our stuff together. We walked out to the front of the studio to wait for Mom.

Jane trailed after us. "I'm really sorry."

"Don't worry about it," Jessica said.

"It wasn't your fault," I told her.

"Do you think our friends were watching?" Jessica asked me.

"Yes," I said.

"School is going to be awful tomorrow," Jessica said.

I nodded.

Nobody said anything for a few minutes.

"Jessica?" I finally whispered. "Um . . . I'm sorry for everything I said."

"Me too," Jessica said.

"Are we friends again?" I asked.

"Sure," Jessica said. "You're my best friend." Tears came to her eyes. "You're my *only* friend."

CHAPTER 11

True Friends

"What are they staring at?" Jessica whispered.

"Us," I replied.

Jessica and I had just climbed onto the bus on Tuesday morning. A few of the kids were staring at us. I heard a lot of whispering.

"Just don't pay attention," Jessica told me.

I nodded, took a deep breath, and started down the aisle. Jessica was right behind me.

"Great show!" one of Steven's friends yelled.

"Too bad it was your last," Jerry McAllister added.

The boys laughed so hard, they almost fell into the aisle.

Jessica and I walked by Caroline Pearce. She was sitting on the aisle. The seat next to her was empty. But Caroline didn't slide over to make room.

I saw two empty seats together. They were next to Todd. If we sat there, he would probably yell at us.

But then Todd waved. "I saved two seats," he called.

"Thanks," Jessica said after she sat down.

"You're the best," I added.

"I thought you thought I was a baby," Todd said.

"You're not," I told him. "I'm sorry I said you were."

"Well, then I'm sorry I said you were a snake," Todd said.

"That's OK," I said. "I asked for it."
Todd smiled.

I felt much better.

I made a decision. I was going to tell *everyone* I was sorry. It didn't matter if it was bad for my image. I wasn't a television star anymore. I didn't have to worry.

The bus pulled up at school. I jumped off.

"Where are you going?" Jessica yelled.

"To make up with my friends," I told her. I ran into Mrs. Otis's room. Julie and Amy were looking at our class hamsters, Thumbelina and Tinkerbell.

"Hi, you guys!"

Julie and Amy traded looks. "Hi," they both said. But they weren't smiling.

"I just told Todd I was sorry," I said. "He's not mad at me anymore."

"That's good," Amy said.

"Can we play together at recess?" I asked.

"I don't know," Julie said.

"Please?" I asked. "We can play whatever you like. And you can go first."

Julie smiled. "I don't care what we play."

"We could play tag half the time, and hopscotch the other half," Amy suggested.

"That sounds great," I said.

Julie agreed.

I walked over to my desk.

Jessica was already sitting down. Lila's desk is next to Jessica's. Ellen sits on the other side of Lila. Ellen and Lila were talking to each other. But they weren't talking to Jessica. Jessica was pretending not to notice them. She looked unhappy.

"Why don't you tell Lila you're sorry?" I whispered to Jessica.

"I want to," Jessica whispered back. "But I'm afraid."

Just then, Lila tapped Jessica on the shoulder.

We turned around.

"I saw your show yesterday," Lila said. "It looks like your days on TV are over." She looked happy.

Jessica clenched her fists.

"We don't know yet," I said quickly.

Jessica took a deep breath. "Listen," she said. "I'm sorry I told everyone about your night-light. And—and I cheat at hopscotch sometimes, too."

Lila was surprised. She didn't say anything for a moment. "It's too bad Linda is so mad at you," she finally said.

"Let's make up," Jessica suggested.

"OK," Lila agreed.

"Great," Jessica said.

But then Ellen elbowed Lila. "Don't make up with her! She acts like she's better than everyone else."

"Jessica and I both acted that way," I said. "But we're sorry. And we should have listened to your idea for the show."

Ellen looked satisfied.

Jessica grinned at me. "Now everyone is friends again."

"Almost," I agreed. I got up and walked over to Andy's desk.

"What do *you* want?" he asked.

"To say I'm sorry," I said. "Your bug collection isn't boring. I think it's pretty cool."

Andy still looked angry.

"Especially that new beetle," I added.

"She's a beauty," Andy agreed.

"No," I said. "She's an ugly!"

Andy laughed.

CHAPTER 12

A Star Is Born

"Pass the popcorn," Jessica said.

At four o'clock on Wednesday, Amy, Julie, Lila, Ellen, Jessica, and I were in the Suttons' den. The television was tuned to Channel 31. *It's the Jane Show!* was going to start any minute.

"Are you going back to the show?" Julie asked.

I shrugged. "Only if Linda asks us."

"If Jane does a good job, we're finished," Jessica said.

"Then I hope she messes up," Ellen said.

We all laughed. But I didn't really want Jane to mess up. She was too nice.

It turned out that Jane was really talented. She told jokes. She showed us her goldfish. She put on her favorite record, and we all danced. Jane could even juggle!

"That is so cool!" Jessica said.

When the show was over, everyone thought it had been great.

"That was really good!" I exclaimed.

"Our TV career is over," Jessica said.

Jessica and I were eating our snack the next afternoon when the phone rang.

"Girls!" Mom called. "It's Linda for you!"

Jessica made a face. "You talk to her."

"OK," I agreed. I ran to the phone and picked it up. "Hello?"

"Jessica?" Linda asked.

"It's Elizabeth," I said. "Jessica is standing right here."

"I have a sack of mail for you girls," Linda reported. "The viewers want you back. Be at the studio at the usual time tomorrow!"

"All right!" I told Linda. "See you then."

Jessica's eyes were round. "What did she say?"

"She wants us back!"

Jessica and I jumped up and down and squealed.

"This time we'll have the best show ever," I said.

"Definitely!"

"But we have to be careful," I added. "We can't say anything bad about our friends."

"Right." Jessica was beginning to look worried. "So what do you want to do on the show tomorrow?"

"I don't know," I admitted. "But we'd better plan every second, just to be safe."

"Let's go upstairs and make out a list," Jessica said.

"OK," I agreed glumly. Being on TV was hard. I didn't want to make lists every day.

"You know what?" I said to Jessica. "I don't think I want to go back."

Jessica looked happy. "Really? I don't want to, either!"

"You don't?"

Jessica shook her head. "It's a big pain. Let's call Linda and tell her."

We found the number for the studio. I dialed. I thought Linda would be mad when we quit. But all she said was, "Fine. I'll call Jane."

The phone rang again a few minutes later. I picked it up.

"It's Jane," I told Jessica.

"I'll go downstairs."

85

"Jessica is getting the phone in the kitchen," I told Jane.

"Hello!" Jessica said.

"Hi," Jane said. "I wanted to thank you for my big break. I'm so excited. But I wish I had a twin sister. It's hard when you don't have anyone to talk to."

"Don't worry," I told her. "You have lots of experience. You'll be great."

"Thanks!" Jane said. "So, do you guys have any ideas for my second show?"

"Just one," I told her.

"What?"

"Don't talk about me!"

"I'll double that," Jessica added.

That evening, my family went out to dinner at an Italian restaurant. We had spaghetti and meatballs with garlic bread. Yum!

"I have good news," Mom announced after we ordered.

Dad was smiling. He already knew the news.

"What is it?" I asked.

"Tell me!" Jessica yelled.

Steven was too busy eating to say anything.

"I just got a big job," Mom told us. "I'm going to pick out new wallpaper, tablecloths, napkins, and dishes for this restaurant!"

Mom studies interior design. She is very good at making a room look pretty. That's important in a restaurant.

"Congratulations," Jessica said.

I felt very proud of my mom, and I told her so.

"That's cool," Steven said, in between bites of garlic bread.

"Thank you." Mom looked happy. "There's only one problem. This project must be finished quickly. I'm going to be working very hard. I won't be around when you kids get home from school. So I hired a baby-sitter to watch you."

Steven groaned. "I'm too old for a baby-sitter."

"We've already made the arrangements," Dad said. "It's too late to argue."

"Which baby-sitter?" I asked.

"She's a new baby-sitter—you haven't met her yet," Mom told us. "Amy's mother gave me her phone number. I spoke to her this afternoon, and she sounds very nice. Her name is Molly."

"Don't worry about us," I told Mom.

Jessica nodded. "We'll be fine."

"I'm sure we'll like Molly," I added. But inside I didn't feel so sure.

Will Elizabeth, Jessica, and Steven like their new baby-sitter? Find out in Sweet Valley Kids #56, JESSICA PLAYS CUPID.

SIGN UP FOR THE SWEET VALLEY HIGH® FAN CLUB!

Hey, girls! Get all the gossip on Sweet Valley High's® most popular teenagers when you join our fantastic Fan Club! As a member, you'll get all of this really cool stuff:

- Membership Card with your own personal Fan Club ID number
- A Sweet Valley High® Secret Treasure Box
- Sweet Valley High® Stationery
- Official Fan Club Pencil (for secret note writing!)
- Three Bookmarks
- A "Members Only" Door Hanger
- Two Skeins of J. & P. Coats® Embroidery Floss with flower barrette instruction leaflet
- Two editions of *The Oracle* newsletter
- Plus exclusive Sweet Valley High® product offers, special savings, contests, and much more!

Be the first to find out what Jessica & Elizabeth Wakefield are up to by joining the Sweet Valley High® Fan Club for the one-year membership fee of only $6.25 each for U.S. residents, $8.25 for Canadian residents (U.S. currency). Includes shipping & handling.

Send a check or money order (do not send cash) made payable to "Sweet Valley High® Fan Club" along with this form to:

SWEET VALLEY HIGH® FAN CLUB, BOX 3919-B, SCHAUMBURG, IL 60168-3919

NAME_____
(Please print clearly)

ADDRESS_____

CITY_____ STATE_____ ZIP_____
(Required)

AGE_____ BIRTHDAY_____ /_____ /_____

Offer good while supplies last. Allow 6-8 weeks after check clearance for delivery. Addresses without ZIP codes cannot be honored. Offer good in USA & Canada only. Void where prohibited by law.

LCI-1383-193